In the Time of Dinosaurs

PART I

Look for other **ANIMORPHS**®
titles by K.A. Applegate:

In the Time of Dinosaurs PART I

K.A. Applegate

AN
APPLE
PAPERBACK

SCHOLASTIC INC.
New York Toronto London Auckland Sydney

Cover illustration by David B. Mattingly

ISBN 0-590-02357-8

12 11 10 9 8 7 6 5 4 3   8 9/9 0 1 2 3/0

Printed in the U.S.A.   40

First Scholastic printing, June 1998

For Michael and Jake

In the Time of Dinosaurs

PART I

CHAPTER 1

Marco

My name is Marco. And I'm the idiot who happened to be watching the news on TV, and happened to see the story about the nuclear submarine that went down.

Do you ever wish you could just learn to keep your mouth shut? I do. At least in this case I did. Because if I'd just kept my mouth shut, I wouldn't have ended up trying to suck air through my blowhole in the middle of a raging storm that kept dropping thirty-foot waves on my head.

But maybe I should back up. Maybe I should explain why I had a blowhole in the first place.

I'll make this quick: Things are happening here on good old planet Earth. Things most people would never dream of. Things that if you told people they'd say, "Yeah, right. Want to try on this straitjacket?"

We are being invaded. Not by spaceships from outer space firing ray guns. I mean, yes, from spaceships, but mostly the Yeerks don't use a lot of ray guns.

The Yeerks are a parasitic species. Like tapeworms or lice or certain gym coaches who think you can't play basketball just because you are somewhat not tall.

But Yeerks don't crawl on top of your head like lice. They crawl inside your head. A slug like a big snail slithers into your ear, oozes into your brain, flattens itself out, sinks into all the cracks in your brain, and from that point on, controls you. It can even force you to listen to Kenny G.

Actually, it's not funny. I tend to make jokes, especially about things that bother me. And the Yeerks bother me. One of those people who has been enslaved by the Yeerks is my mother. We thought she was dead. She's not. At least I think she's not. When I last saw her she was still alive. Trying to destroy me and my friends, as a matter of fact.

Which is a lot worse than just being grounded.

Anyway, there are the Yeerks, this parasitic species that rampages throughout the galaxy looking for new host bodies. They control the Gedds, a species from their home planet. They control the Hork-Bajir and the Taxxons. And their target now is Earth and humans.

What does this have to do with me having a blowhole? Well, there's another species in on this with us. The Andalites. The Andalites are stretched thin trying to resist the Yeerks. An Andalite task force got hammered in orbit above Earth. One of them, Prince Elfangor, made it to Earth and happened to crash near my friends and me. He gave us the Andalite morphing power. The ability to absorb DNA from any animal, and then actually, literally *become* that animal.

We use that power to resist the Yeerks. "We" being Jake, who is our prematurely middle-aged, fearless more-or-less leader; Cassie, our animal expert and tree-hugging environmental wacko; Rachel, Jake's fabulously beautiful but totally insane cousin; Tobias, who's a mouse-eating bird; the Cinnabon-chomping Andalite scorpion-boy we call Ax; and me, Marco, the sensitive, sensible, smart, and good-looking one.

Also modest. And honest.

And did I mention cute?

Anyway, I was hanging out with my dad around noon on a rainy Saturday, slumped down in the easy chair, staring at the TV, wondering if I had the energy to go into the kitchen to get more Doritos, when the news flash came on.

A nuclear sub was reported to have developed

reactor problems. It was feared sunk. Rescue ships and divers were on the scene, but the storm was making it hard for them. They couldn't find the sub, which could be dousing everyone on board with radiation.

"Oh, man," I groaned.

"Yeah," my dad agreed. He was slumped on the couch wondering if he had the energy to go to the kitchen and get his Cheez Puffs.

"Um . . ." I said.

"Are you going to the kitchen?" he asked hopefully.

I sighed. "Actually, I just remembered I'm supposed to help Jake with some work over at his house."

"Oh. You'll miss the game," he said. "So before you go, could you grab me the bag of Cheez Puffs? And a soda? And a pillow? And give me the remote control."

I carried about twenty-four items to my dad, then took off out into the rain to walk to Jake's house. I had to tell him about the sub. I don't know why, I just had to. I guess I thought we could possibly help.

Thirty minutes later, the six of us were assembled on a wet beach. There was absolutely no one in sight. No lifeguards. No little old ladies collecting shells. I mean, it was really raining. We were all soaked through and had wet sand caking our shoes. All except Rachel, who I swear has some magic ability to repel dirt, mud, and rainwater.

"Well, we have privacy, that's for sure," Jake said, looking around.

"What are we going to do with our outer clothing and shoes?" Cassie wondered.

See, we can't morph clothing and shoes. Just things that are skintight. I was wearing bike shorts and a way-too-small, totally uncool T-shirt under my clothes. Those I could morph.

"I've said it before, I'll say it again," I said. "We have got to do something about these funky morphing outfits. We are a disgrace to super-heroes. Can you imagine us ever being in a comic book alongside Spider-Man? We'd look like the Clampetts."

"The what?" Cassie asked.

"You know, the Beverly Hillbillies."

"Marco, you do realize that Spider-Man isn't real, right?" Rachel asked. "And even if he was, I don't know what fabric that outfit of his is made from. Never bags at the knees or elbows. I mean, come on."

"We'd better get going before someone shows up," Jake said glumly. Jake hates dark, overcast days. It makes him grumpy.

We stripped off our outer clothes and shoes and stuffed them into a backpack. We stuck the backpack in one of the blue trash barrels they had along the beach.

"Maybe we'll get lucky this time and they won't pick up the trash today," Cassie said.

"Yeah, it'd be a shame to lose those jeans of yours," Rachel said. "If your legs shrink five inches those jeans would almost fit."

Rachel and Cassie are best friends. But they don't agree on the importance of clothes.

<Come on,> Tobias called down from above. <There are guys out there who might be dying. Let's just get it over with already!>

Floating over our heads was Tobias, a red-tailed hawk. A wet red-tailed hawk. We heard his thought-speak in our heads. We also knew why he was anxious. Tobias does not like the water. But he was trying to act all macho about it.

We waded into the water. Jake, Cassie, Rachel, and me. And Ax. Ax was in his disturbingly attractive human morph. As opposed to his disturbingly, disturbing true Andalite body. He had to return to his own form before he could go into another morph. He'd picked up his newest morph at The Gardens — with Cassie's help, of course. Tobias had to morph straight from his hawk shape. Which, as you can guess, is not all that fun, since a hawk in the surf is pretty helpless.

I swam out a ways with the others. Tobias

looked around once more with his hawk eyes and pronounced the beach definitely empty. Then he sighed heavily and plunged into the water.

I focused my mind on the DNA inside me. I formed the picture of the dolphin in my head.

And I began to change.

Now you know how I got a blowhole.

CHAPTER 2

Cassie

I love being a dolphin. How can you *not* love it?

I'm not crazy about morphing insects. Especially the mindless little automatons like termites and ants. But I'm convinced that dolphins have souls. Or maybe it's just some arrangement of DNA-based characteristics that make them seem that way to humans. But whatever it is, whether it's something mystical or something real, I like it.

We were in the surf, breasting the waves and staggering against the flow. When the cold water was up to my chest I pushed off and swam. It wasn't easy fighting the waves. Humans are not very strong in the water.

As I dog-paddled, I began to morph. My fingers stretched out longer and longer. A webbing grew between them, like a duck's feet. My arm bones shrank and drew this webbed hand toward my body till it was clearly a fin and not a hand any longer.

My legs softened. Like overcooked spaghetti, they twined together and melted into the long tail of the dolphin. At the same time my feet twisted outward and thinned to become the tail flukes.

Then, as I gasped and spit out mouthfuls of salt water, my flat human mouth and face began to bulge outward. It was like something out of a cartoon. As if I were made of Silly Putty and someone was stretching my face outward.

My eyes moved to the side and now my vision was largely filled with my own grinning dolphin snout.

More dolphin than human now, I sucked in a last lungful of air through my mouth. When I exhaled, it went out through the blowhole that had appeared where the back of my neck had been.

I dove below the churning surface. I was still in shallow water so I could see the sand and gravel and shells being tugged to and fro by the water.

Humans may prefer shallow water, but it makes dolphins uneasy. So I kicked my powerful tail and headed away from shore.

Think about the happiest day you've ever had in your life. Think of how you feel on a sunny day, with no school and no chores, your allowance fresh in your pocket and some really fun thing awaiting you. That's exactly what it feels like to be a dolphin.

Then, to all that good feeling, add this sensation of power, ease, of being the perfectly adapted creature in the perfect place.

<Come on, guys!> I yelled, giddy and goofy on the sheer joy of being a dolphin in the sea.

And they came. All of them felt the same way. We were on a serious mission. But that didn't mean we couldn't have fun.

We raced out to sea, surfacing to deliberately plow into the rising walls of waves. We hurried, but we played the whole way.

And then we began to see the helicopters chattering overhead and the Navy ships patrolling back and forth across the sea. The waves were high, the winds, too. When we surfaced it was in the valleys between waves. We'd blow out our stale breath and suck in fresh air, letting the gray waves lift us up so we could see.

<We must be near where they think it is,> Jake said.

<Is anyone else sucking salt water every time they try to breathe?> Marco asked. <Is that good for you?>

<We *are* in the ocean, Marco,> Rachel pointed out. <There's bound to be water in the ocean.>

<Fine, but do we have to be out here in the middle of a storm?>

<Come on,> Jake said. <Let's go below.>

I nosed downward and kicked. It was much calmer and quieter below the surface. We were in maybe two hundred feet of water. It's hard to tell, but it looked that deep, anyway. I was swimming about fifty feet down and could just barely see the ghostly glimmer of sand far below me. Mostly what I saw was murky blue. Not even many fish.

I fired an echolocation blast from my head. The sound waves spread out, then bounced back. My dolphin brain drew a mental picture of a seabed scarred by a series of deep fissures. I also "saw" divers in the water, and sensors being towed on long cables from the ships above us.

<Even with our echolocation we need to spread out,> Tobias said. <Those fissures are as big as small valleys. The sub could be in one of them.>

<Okay,> Jake agreed. <But everyone stay within thought-speak range of the person on your left and right.>

Easier said than done. You ever try and swim while keeping in line with dolphins on your left and right? Plus we had to surface to breathe, and each time we did the waves would push us forward or back.

Rachel was on my right. Ax on my left. We advanced across the ocean floor, blasting the water with our ultrasonic sound waves.

It had taken forty-five minutes of hard swimming to reach the site. We couldn't go beyond two hours in morph. Not unless we wanted to spend the rest of our lives as dolphins.

Forty-five minutes to get there. Forty-five to get back to shore. That only left thirty minutes to search. Not enough.

But twenty minutes later I saw, or felt, a strange picture in my head. <Hey! Ax, Rachel. I think I got something.>

I fired a new echolocation blast and "listened" carefully. Yes, something weird. Something definitely weird. Something too "hard."

<Yeah. I have something,> I said. <Rachel, aim a little to your left. Ax, just a hair to your right.>

In a few seconds, Rachel said, <Nothing. I'm not getting anything.>

<I am,> Ax said. <A hard, angular object that appears to be jutting up from the seabed. No, from one of the fissures.>

<I'll take a look,> I said. <It could be just some piece of junk or garbage.>

I shot to the surface, filled my lungs, and

12

went down. Down and down, till even my dolphin body began to feel the water pressure.

I kept firing echolocating bursts. And then I was certain. It rose just a few feet from the fissure. But if I recalled my submarine war movies, it was a periscope. The sub's commander must have extended it in the desperate hope that someone would see it.

Someone had. Although not exactly the someone he'd expected.

CHAPTER 3

Jake

We'd found the sub. Now the question was: How could we get the Navy divers to find it?

<Kidnap one of them,> Rachel suggested.

Rachel almost always likes the direct approach. And in this case, she was right. We needed to get this done with fast. We needed to wrap this up and bail.

<Okay,> I said, <we kidnap a diver.>

<What?> Marco said. <You're listening to *Rachel*?>

<She happens to be right,> I said. <Let's go. But don't hurt the person, okay?>

It was easy to find a diver. Their wet-suited bodies and stream of bubbles showed up nice and clear on echolocation.

14

The diver ignored us as we drew near. We were just a pod of dolphins swimming by. We weren't what she was interested in.

I swam around behind her. The others followed.

<Okay, now, we can't help but scare the poor woman, but be as gentle as you can be,> I said. <Grab a leg or an arm. Rachel, help me push.>

One thing you can say about dolphins: There is nothing they can't do in the water. The six of us moved like a well-drilled acrobatic team or something. Hand, leg, hand, leg, we had the diver before she knew what was happening. The others lightly gripped the wetsuit with their dolphin teeth.

"Mblo blo blm blmo!" She yelled. At least that's what it sounded like.

Rachel dug her nose in the small of the woman's back. I nosed her neck, and together the six of us propelled her through the water, almost standing upright, at a speed that must have seemed pretty amazing to her.

She struggled, of course. I think for a moment she thought we were sharks. I could see wide, scared eyes through her face mask when she turned to look back.

But maybe she'd heard stories about dolphins helping drowning people. Or maybe she just liked dolphins. Maybe it was just so obvious we were on a mission. After a few seconds, she relaxed.

We let her go and I swam up and offered a dorsal fin. She took it. Cassie came up on her other side. And now she cooperated with us, holding on to our dorsal fins as we raced more easily ahead.

We stopped directly over the sub. The diver couldn't see it since it was way below us. But we made a nice show of racing down, then back up, so she'd know what we were doing.

Unfortunately, all this took time. Too much time. We had no choice but to demorph in the open sea.

We swam half a mile away from the search area and demorphed. Bad for most of us. Worse for Tobias, wallowing with waterlogged feathers in salt water. Ax, in his own body, could swim quite well.

We remorphed as soon as we could. And now, with plenty of time, we went back to the site. We had to make sure the divers were there.

<Hey, these guys work fast,> Tobias said when we got back to the site.

A small submersible was already pulling away from the submarine. I guess it was some kind of rescue vehicle for taking people off sunken submarines.

We hovered above the sunken sub. It was

wedged deep in the fissure. It was hard to see how they'd ever get it out.

<May I ask a question?> Ax said. <What is the purpose of these submarines? This is a very large craft for simply looking at the seabed?>

A second small submersible was on its way down. It was zipping along. And the divers were all heading for the surface.

I winced. The purpose of this kind of submarine was a little embarrassing to explain to an alien. <Actually, Ax, it's a military submarine. See the rows of hatches along the back? It's a nuclear missile sub. There's a missile under each of those hatches. Armed with a nuclear warhead.>

<Ah. I see.>

<It's deterrence. You know, in case the enemy uses nukes on us, we have these safe on our subs,> Marco explained.

<What enemy?>

<Well . . . okay, we don't exactly have one right now,> I said, feeling fairly idiotic. <But we used to. And we may get one again.>

<We're shopping all the sales,> Marco said brightly. <Enemies "R" Us, EnemyMart, J.C. Enemy. Don't worry, we'll find one.>

<Are those guys all in a hurry or what?> Rachel asked.

<I was noticing the same thing,> Cassie said.

<And look, up above. The ships are all leaving the area. Going in all directions.>

I looked down. The rescue vehicle was already pulling away from the sub. But instead of heading up to the surface, it was simply racing away. Like it was desperate to put some distance between it and the sub.

<I suddenly have a very bad feeling about this,> Tobias said.

<Outta here!> I yelled.

We turned and took off. We powered our tails and tore through the water like torpedoes.

The rescue vehicle was a quarter mile ahead of us. I lost sight of it when we shot to the surface to breathe.

Up, suck in air, down and swim, and up, suck in air, down and swim. It was slower going on the surface, but we needed to breathe because we were straining every muscle in our bodies.

<This is probably stupid,> Rachel said. <I mean, what do we think is going to —>

Flash! A light so bright it seemed to burn right through me.

WHAAAAAAM! The shock wave hit us.

I tumbled through a world that was being torn apart at the seams. And then that world went black.

CHAPTER 4

Rachel

I don't know how long I was unconscious. But when I came to I was on the surface of the water. I was lolling there like some kind of dead fish.

First thought: *Where are the others?*

Second thought: *How long have I been in morph?*

<Cassie! Tobias! Jake!> I yelled in thought-speak.

No answer. I moved my tail and flippers. Okay, at least I wasn't injured. I dove below the surface and looked around. The water was clearer than it had been. Strange, given the fact that a nuclear warhead had just exploded.

<Marco! Ax!>

<I was wondering when you'd get around to calling *me*,> Marco answered.

He glided up beside me.

<Have you seen any of the others?>

<No. But I was knocked out.>

I fired an echolocation burst. Fish. A pair of distant whales. No dolphins. Although if they were floating on the surface they might not show up.

<I have an idea,> Marco said. <We dive down, then look up. They should be silhouetted against the sun.>

<Good idea. Only it's raining. There's no . . .> I'd been about to say there was no sun. But the golden rays were piercing the water around me. <Must have cleared up. Man, we may have been out a long time.>

We dove down deep. We looked up. And there, outlined against the sun, were four tapered shapes.

<Come on,> I said and shot toward them. I bonked one of them with my nose.

<Hey! What? What?> Tobias yelped. <Jeez! You scared me to death. Good grief, I thought you were one of those lousy wildcats.>

<Tobias, only *you* would wake up suddenly and worry about wildcats,> Marco said.

<Try sleeping in a tree in the woods,> he grumbled. <You'll worry about them, too.>

We nudged each of the others. Ax and Jake revived. Cassie revived, too. But she woke up screaming in pain.

<Ahhh! Ahhh!>

That's when we noticed the blood leaking from her eyes and blowhole.

<Oh, oh, it hurts!>

<Demorph!> Jake yelled.

<Trying . . . trying . . . oh, oh!>

Gradually the gray rubbery flesh melted away and a human girl emerged. As she demorphed, the dolphin's pain was left behind. I nuzzled in close, giving her a dorsal fin to hang onto.

"Wow, that really hurt," she said calmly, once her human mouth was back in place. She looked around. "Why is the water so calm? Why is it sunny?" She lifted herself up a foot out of the water, using Jake and me as support.

Then she settled back. "Um . . . am I awake?"

<Of course.>

"And this isn't a dream?"

<Can't be a dream,> Marco said. <There's not a single *Baywatch* girl around. Carmen is always there when I dream.>

"You're sure this is reality?" Cassie asked before I could make a crushing remark to Marco about the total impossibility of Carmen Electra ever even looking at him.

<Cassie, it's not a dream,> Jake said.

"Okay. Then why is there a volcano over there?"

No one said anything for a few seconds. Then all at once we dove down under, leaving Cassie floundering and yelling, "Hey!"

I dove down twenty feet, turned and powered my way straight up. I exploded from the water, smooth and sleek as a missile. I shot up into the air, up where I could see beyond the tops of the short, choppy waves.

I took a look. Then, too stunned to line up for a dive, I belly flopped. The first dolphin in history to belly flop. <There's a volcano over there! There's an actual volcano! We don't have a volcano. I would have noticed that.>

<That was a definite volcano,> Tobias agreed.

<Is it some weird effect from the explosion?> Jake asked. <Like maybe setting off that bomb in the fissure caused some kind of sudden eruption?>

"We have to get back! People could be hurt!"

<Something is way wrong here,> I said. <Volcanoes don't just suddenly erupt. Besides, look how high that thing was. That takes hundreds of years of lava and ash building up.>

<How do you know anything about volcanoes?> Jake demanded. <Did we do volcanoes in school?>

<No it was . . . some other place,> I mumbled. But they all just waited. Waited to hear how I knew about volcanoes. <Oh, all right. It was the *Magic School Bus*, okay? They went into a volcano.>

<Excuse me,> Ax said politely. <But something very large is coming toward us. A pair of creatures of some sort. I just echolocated them.>

<A pair of whales,> I said, dismissing it. <I saw them earlier. I think we need to haul back to land and see what —>

<Not whales,> Ax said.

<Who cares? Maybe you missed it, Ax, but we have a volcano — *a volcano!* — right about where all our houses should be! Let's get going. Cassie, you need to —>

"Uh . . . what is that?" Cassie asked. She was staring hard, but she started to morph back into dolphin.

<What?>

"*That!*"

I turned to follow the direction of her stare. We all turned.

It rose ten feet from the water. A very long neck. Like a gray-green giraffe. On the end of that neck was a sculpted, streamlined head about two feet long. And coming up, right behind it, was another tall neck and head.

<No way,> Tobias whispered.

<What is that, the Loch Ness monster?!> Marco cried.

<It's Visser Three in morph!> I said. <No, wait, can't be. There are two of them.>

<No *way*!> Tobias said again.

<They're coming after us!> Cassie said.

<As I said,> Ax said smugly, <*not* whales.>

CHAPTER 5

Tobias

I knew what it was. Or at least I knew what it looked like. But I wasn't about to say anything. If I was wrong, Marco would tease me about it till the day I died. Besides, it was impossible. Totally impossible.

So I didn't say anything.

But oh, man, I hauled my dolphin tail out of there.

<They're too fast,> Jake said. <Man, they're fast!>

We were plowing up the now-placid water. We were going flat out. But the creatures were gaining on us. And the whole time in my head I was going, *No way, no* way.

And yet with each glance at those long necks, with each flash of those snake heads, I became more convinced.

The creatures were no more than a hundred feet back.

<We can't outrun them,> Jake said grimly. <We either have to split up or fight.>

<Fight!> Rachel said. <They're just some kind of big squid or something probably. Let's get them!>

I liked Rachel even before I became a hawk. But now I really like her. She could be a bird of prey. She'd be a natural.

But she was wrong this time.

<Split up,> I said. <I don't think we can beat them.>

<We haven't tried yet,> she said.

<You don't understand. Look, I know this will sound crazy, but —>

SHWOOOOSH!

Coming up from below. Like some weird, massively oversized dolphin. Forty . . . fifty feet long! An impossibly huge jaw open wide.

We'd been watching the creatures chasing us. All I had time to see of this new threat was the flash of teeth.

<Aaaahhhh!> It had me. No time to move. Up, up, up I went! High into the air, trapped in those massive jaws as it broke the surface.

It tossed me up. Just like I'd seen seabirds do with a fish. Tossed me up, opened its massive jaws, and swallowed me whole.

I was being swallowed!

I was unconscious, then conscious again, then unconscious.

I hit water. No, not water! Too warm. Hot. Burning! My skin was burning!

I was blind. Deaf, except for the sound of churning. And the steady bass drum of a heart beating.

Then, something else beside me. My dolphin sense knew. It was another dolphin. <Who is that?>

<It's me!> an enraged voice cried.

<Rachel!>

<Who did you expect? Jonah? We have to get out of this thing. Ahhhh! My skin is itching and burning.>

<Stomach acid,> I said. <It's digesting us.>

<It's not digesting *me*!> Rachel said. <I'm gonna morph! I'm tearing a hole out of here.>

<You have to pass through human to morph,> I said. <The stomach acid!>

<No choice.>

I could already feel her changing. I felt human fingers pressed against me in the gnashing, enclosed space. She was right. No other choice. And I wasn't going to let her do it alone.

I had very few morphs available to me. And only one that would help here. But first I had to revert to bird form.

Something like a rock was in the stomach. It was grinding against me with the movements of the stomach wall. And as I lost the tough hide of a dolphin and regained the fragile hollow bones of my own hawk body, the beating became deadly.

Even Rachel's body was crushing me, as her elbows and fists and knees were shoved against me, time and again.

But all that was nothing compared to one simple fact: I couldn't breathe.

Suffocating!

<Air!> I moaned.

Rachel couldn't answer. She was human again. But I knew she must be suffocating, too.

My left wing was broken. My tail was a mess. I was wracked with pain. But none of that mattered because I was going down now. Sinking and swirling down a long, black well.

Too late to morph again. I knew it. I was done.

And my last conscious thought was a flash of myself, years earlier, back when I was still completely human. I saw myself playing with the little plastic figurine — a plastic toy model of the animal whose belly I was in. A booklet had come with the figurine. I'd memorized all the facts in that booklet.

<They were wrong,> I thought as my mind shut down. <It's bigger than they said.>

CHAPTER 6

Jake

<It has Rachel and Tobias!> Cassie screamed.

I knew. I'd been on the surface when the monster had snatched them up and tossed them down its throat. But I couldn't think about that. I still had three people with me. I had to save them.

The long-necked creatures were behind us, the larger one in front. Which would eat us?

<Everyone dive!> I said.

<What about — ?> Marco began.

<Do it!> I roared.

Down we went. Down fifty, sixty, seventy feet. The monsters were like ships overhead. The two long-necked ones started to dive after us. Then they hesitated. The larger creature, the one that had gotten Rachel and Tobias, was closing in.

<Now! While they're arguing over who gets to eat us,> I said. <Let's get out of here!>

<We can't leave Rachel and Tobias,> Cassie said.

<Can you beat that thing, Cassie?> I demanded. <You want to stay here and try? Sooner or later those creatures will decide who we belong to. We have to run while they're fighting over us.>

<Rachel!> Cassie cried in thought-speak. <Rachel! Can you hear me? Rachel!>

<Now, Cassie! Marco, Ax, get her!>

Marco and Ax each bit down on a flipper and dragged Cassie away.

<Let me go! Rachel! Rachel! RACHEL!>

I felt sick inside. Mad at Cassie, scared, beaten, and for some reason even mad at Rachel and Tobias. But mostly I felt sick. What was happening?

We swam away as fast as we could move. I heard a screeching roar of rage reverberating through the water. The monsters were fighting.

We swam toward shore. And after a while Cassie swam on her own.

The sea floor beneath us sloped up and up, rising to meet us. When we were in no more than five feet of water, we began to demorph. I hoped we could do it. I didn't know how long we'd been in morph.

I gratefully resumed my own body. I lifted myself sluggishly out of the water and staggered up the beach. I flopped facedown, then rolled over.

Cassie and Marco came seconds later. Ax took a few extra minutes and appeared in human morph.

"Something is very wrong, Prince Jake," he said.

I didn't answer. Of course something was wrong. Rachel and Tobias were probably dead. So something would always be wrong now. Forever.

"Jake, Ax is right," Marco said. "Get up. Look at this!"

I stood up. Marco, Ax, and Cassie were all staring, openmouthed, across the beach toward the boardwalk.

There was no boardwalk.

No hot dog stands, no Ferris wheel, no video arcades. No buildings at all. No people. Nothing but a line of trees pressing right up against the sand. And off above the trees, the cone of the volcano with a tall plume of smoke.

"This isn't home," Marco said.

"What is going on here?" I wondered. I slogged up the beach toward the trees. I expected to see something behind the trees. But behind the front row of trees were just more trees. Far off, through gaps in the tree trunks, I caught glimpses of an open space. But I was seeing grass and flowers there, not a city.

Marco and Cassie came up behind me.

"Listen," Marco said.

"Listen to what?"

"The quiet. Just the breeze in the trees."

Cassie said, "No seagulls. There are always gulls."

I had noticed something else. "There's no trash. No old soda cans. No candy wrappers. Nothing. I mean, *nothing*."

"So, what happened?" Marco asked. "That explosion blew us halfway around the planet to some desert island somewhere in the middle of nowhere?"

I shrugged. Most of my brain was still focused on Rachel and Tobias. I wasn't tracking. And yet I felt a nagging sense of urgency. A little voice telling me to get it together. A little warning voice telling me we were not safe.

I turned around. "Ax! What are you doing?"

He was about a hundred yards down the beach. "I'm trying to understand something, Prince Jake."

I headed toward him. The sand was darker and rougher than I remembered. But then, who knew where we were? The tracks I saw in the sand seemed to have been made by large birds. I got this sudden, illogical rush, thinking maybe they'd been left by Tobias. They looked like they'd been made by talons.

But of course that was impossible. I had gotten Tobias and Rachel killed. If only I'd been watching ahead instead of looking behind, I could have seen the threat coming. I should have had everyone morph to shark. Then we could have fought.

Should have, should have.

"No footprints," Cassie said. "No human footprints, anyway."

We reached Ax. He was staring toward the trees. I followed the direction of his look. There was a sort of alleyway through the trees. Some were bent aside. Some had the branches on one side broken, hanging limp with dying leaves. Other trees were simply snapped. Broken.

And all along this "alleyway" the top third of the trees seemed to have been stripped of leaves.

Marco stared, too. He bumped into me and shoved me into a hole in the sand. I was going to shove him back, but this was no time to be playing around.

"I am still unfamiliar with some Earth creatures," Ax said. "Cuh-ree-chers. Tell me, what sort of creature can do that?"

"Probably a tornado or something," I said

vaguely. "I've seen things like that on TV when there's been a tornado."

"Ah," Ax said. "Does a tornado have feet?"

I almost smiled. "No. A tornado is a wind storm."

"I see. Then this was not caused by a tornado. Whatever did this has feet."

"How do you know?" Cassie asked.

"Because Prince Jake is standing in one of the footprints."

I looked down. It could have been the footprint of an elephant. Except that the toes were more like claws.

Plus, the print sank at least six inches into the sand.

And oh, yes: It was about four feet across.

CHAPTER 7

Cassie

Jake jumped up out of that footprint like it was filled with rattlesnakes.

We stared at the footprint.

Then we looked up and stared at the alleyway that something had made through the trees.

Then we stared at the way the leaves had been stripped from a lot of the highest branches of the trees.

"Jake, something ate those leaves," I pointed out.

"Those trees are like thirty feet tall," Jake said.

"There are a cluster of these same footprints over there." Ax pointed about ten feet away.

36

"And all across there it's as if the sand has been swept. Swe-put. Swep-tuh."

Jake looked at me. "Cassie, do you know anything that could possibly have this footprint?"

Jake thinks I'm some kind of animal expert. I shook my head. "What it looks like is some very, very large animal came through those woods. It was munching the top leaves of the trees. Like a giraffe would do. Then it hit the water here. It turned around. That's the cluster of prints there. And it has an insanely long tail. That's the swept area. Once it was turned around, it went back the way it came."

"A giraffe?" Jake asked.

"Not a giraffe," I said.

Jake looked a little confused. We all were, but he's the one who gets stuck making the decisions. I felt sorry for him. He'd been right to drag me away from those sea monsters. I should have told him that.

But poor Rachel. Poor Tobias. What was I ever going to do without Rachel? Rachel had been my best friend forever. I couldn't imagine not seeing her every day.

I realized I was crying. I guess I had been, off and on, since we'd dragged up out of the sea.

I felt Jake's arm go around my shoulders. "Don't cry, Cassie. Don't give up on Rachel and

Tobias. You know Rachel. If there's a way to survive, she'll find it."

I wiped my tears. "Yeah. You're right. And we have to focus here."

He took his arm away and suddenly seemed awkward. I think he expected Marco to make some smirky remark. But Marco has a good heart. He knows when to let things go. Besides, I knew Marco was almost as sad as I was.

"What should we do, Prince Jake?" Ax wondered.

"Have I mentioned don't call me prince?" Jake said automatically.

"Yes, Prince Jake, you have."

Jake looked around. "I guess we go that way," he said, pointing to the forest. "But not along *that* path. Whatever crushed those trees and made these tracks, we don't want to run into it. But obviously, wherever we are — some island somewhere, Africa, South America — wherever we are, there have to be people, right? Just not here on the beach. So let's go find them."

I found myself looking back at the sea, at the surf that lapped almost peacefully on the coarse dark sand. Was she still alive somehow? Jake was right: If anyone could get swallowed by a whale — or whatever that thing had been — and survive, it was Rachel.

38

"I caught a glimpse of a clearing way back in the trees," I said. "Could be a village there."

Jake led the way into the trees. The sun was shut out by the tall, spreading branches. There were vines hanging down and crawling up the trunks of trees. And huge ferns so big you could hide in them.

We struck a stream, maybe fifteen feet across. Both banks of the river were lined by magnolias, dogwoods, and massive fig trees.

"This is not anywhere near being home," I said. "This is more like tropical vegetation."

"It's humid enough, that's for sure," Marco complained.

"I wonder if the water's okay to drink?" Jake asked. Then, with a shrug, he dropped to his knees and dipped his hand in. He brought the water to his mouth and sipped.

"I guess we can always get a bunch of shots for whatever disease is in the water," I said. I dropped beside him and tasted the water. The humidity hadn't seemed so bad down by the ocean. But now it was dehydrating me. I was massively thirsty.

"It's probably okay," I said. "Usually running water —"

FWOOOSH!

A huge head exploded from the water.

SNAP!

A jaw six feet long slammed shut with a sound like steel on steel. The jaw snapped shut so close to my face that it grazed my nose.

I leaped back. Fell on my butt. Spun, jumped up, and bolted.

"That was one big honkin' crocodile!" Marco yelled as he ran beside me.

We stopped beneath a huge tree. Four of us, all panting.

"That wasn't right," I gasped.

"Yeah, no kidding," Marco said.

"No, I mean it was too big. The jaw was too long and thin."

"I am really not liking this," Jake muttered. "What were those things in the ocean? What made that footprint? Where on Earth are we that has crocodiles that size? I mean, we've seen crocodiles. That was one way, *way* big croc."

"Prince Jake, I am going to demorph," Ax said.

"Have you been in morph too long?" Jake asked with a frown.

"No. But I am frightened," Ax replied. "I don't want to have to fight in this weak human body."

"Yeah, go ahead," Jake said. "Cassie, I don't mean to hit you with this, but you know more about animals than any of us. Where the — where on Earth are we?"

"I don't know," I admitted. "Giant crocodiles, huge, aggressive whales or whatever, like nothing I've ever even heard of, and something big enough to leave a footprint you could turn into a wading pool. I just don't know."

"Okay, fine," he said, obviously frustrated. "Let's try it another way. Ax, you know more about physics and so on than any of us —"

"More than *any* human," Ax said. He was de-morphing but was still mostly human.

"Whatever. Just tell me how an explosion could have blown us all the way to, I don't know, Madagascar or wherever, without killing us."

"Madagascar?" Marco asked.

"It couldn't," Ax said simply.

"Great. Great. That clears everything up just fine. This is nuts." He sighed. He looked at me and shrugged.

"I don't know," I said. "Maybe when we find some people they can tell us where we are."

We walked on, heading toward the clearing. The forest had become a frightening place to us. Everything was wrong. Out of place somehow, in some way I couldn't quite explain. How had the storm and rain suddenly become humid sunlight? How had we gone into the water off a beach fronted by a boardwalk and come out at a beach fronted by forest?

"Maybe it's all a dream," Marco said, as if

41

he'd been reading my thoughts. "In which case, I'd like to dream about a nice, ice-cold Coke." He held out his hand, curved around an imaginary bottle. "Hmm. So much for the dream theory."

We were almost to the clearing now. I could see bright, buttery sunlight through the trees. But massive ferns blocked my view of the clearing itself.

"Let's get out from under these trees," I said. "We'll think better in the open. And maybe there will be some people."

"Too bad they'll speak Madagascarese," Marco said.

"Shhh!" I froze.

"What?"

"Shhhh! Listen!" A grunting, snuffling sound to our left. Then the sound of greenery being rustled. Then more snuffling. The sound of . . . eating? "Something munching leaves," I said.

"There's been way too much munching already," Marco muttered.

"No, it's okay," I said. "If it eats plants, it won't eat *us*. Could be a cow. If it's a cow, maybe it belongs to someone."

"And if it doesn't belong to anyone, maybe we can eat *it*. I'm starving."

We threaded our way cautiously toward the sound. The closer we got, the more confident I was. Yes, something was grazing. But did cows eat leaves? No. Deer, maybe?

I pushed aside a fern frond. And there it was.

It was perhaps twenty feet long from head to tail. It stood on four elephantlike legs. It had a long neck that made up a third of its length and was balanced by the long tail of equal length. Along its back were bumpy, bony things, like armor plating that only covered that one area.

For about two minutes I don't think one of us drew a breath. We just stared.

"I think it's a baby," I said.

"A baby?" Marco said. "Cassie, it's a dinosaur."

Suddenly.

Crash! Crash! CRASH! CRASH!

From behind us!

"HuuuuRROOOOAAARR!"

The ground shook from the impact of its huge, taloned feet. The blast of its roar shivered the leaves and buckled my knees.

I spun around just in time to see it leap.

It jumped over us like we weren't even there. Jumped over us with its awful, hawklike talons. It landed with one huge foot on the ground and one holding the side of the "little" dinosaur.

Down came the head. That huge square, familiar head.

The Tyrannosaurus opened its massive jaws

and closed them at the base of the baby dinosaur's neck.

I didn't know what was happening. My mind was gone. Gone in out-of-control terror.

We ran.

CHAPTER 8
Rachel

I was human! A human gasping for air inside the belly of the creature.

My lungs were screaming and heaving. I was blind. My skin was burning. I was being pummeled, crushed, smashed, beaten.

I was getting mad.

I knew Tobias was there, too, but I had no idea where. He wasn't thought-speaking.

Morph! I told myself. But already I was weakening. The human body can't last long without air.

I tried to focus. But my head was swirling. I wanted to just give up. Why fight it? I was done for.

Not yet, you're not done for, Rachel, I told

myself. *Not yet. I might not survive, but by God, I was going to deal with this creature before I went down.*

From far off I could sense the changes occurring. I knew I was growing. But too weak . . . too weak . . . no time . . . no time. And once I dug out I'd find water. Not air.

Air. I needed air. Some nagging part of my brain kept saying, "Lungs!"

I felt like saying, "Yes, I know. I'm suffocating. I know all about my lungs. They hurt. They're heaving, gasping, crying for air."

And I swear, as I swirled down into the darkness, there came a voice, clear as a bell in my head. My own voice, but from outside of my own head.

"No, you idiot," it said. "Not *your* lungs. Duh."

It was the weirdest thing. But suddenly I could see myself clearly. I even knew that I was halfway morphed. I had blond hair on my head and coarse brown fur on my face. I was crushed inside the gizzard of the beast. A tiny, crumpled bundle of feathers was pressed against me.

I could see it all. But better than that, I could see what the voice meant. I was enclosed in a cage made up of massive ribs. But right there, just a foot away, was air.

I drew back my massive paw. The paw of a

grizzly bear. A paw that could destroy a man with a single, backhanded swipe. I drew that paw back and I extended my wicked, hooked claws, and I thrust that paw straight out. I twisted and pushed. The twist ripped and the power of the thrust dug my paw deep into the creature's insides.

"HREEEEE-UH!"

I heard its scream. It reverberated through the flesh that pressed all around me.

I thrust and twisted.

"HREEEEE-UH!"

Another scream. A spasm that wracked the body so powerfully it almost knocked me out.

But I was not so easily crushed now. I was no longer human. I had finished morphing the grizzly bear. And not even this sea monster could digest a grizzly bear.

With my last ounce of strength, I thrust and twisted.

SHWOOOOOSH!

Air!

Air poured in. I gasped at it. Air!

I had done it. I had ripped a hole out of the gizzard and penetrated the creature's lungs.

<Tobias! Breathe! There's air!>

I went back to work, ripping now with both huge paws. Digging downward to avoid the ribs.

Suddenly water gushed in. Salt water. Cold

and wonderful. I kicked and clawed the opening till it was bigger. Then I tumbled out. I hit bottom. I looked up, dazed and disoriented.

The creature had beached itself. I was in no more than five or six feet of water. I stood up, my huge bear head broke the surface, and I reared up on my hind legs.

Tobias was fluttering weakly in the water. I grabbed him up as gently as I could with bear paws. I lumbered toward shore and set him down on dry land.

<Tobias, are you okay?>

<Do I *look* okay?> he asked.

<Well . . .>

<Busted wing. Feathers a mess. Half my tail feathers ripped out or eaten away by stomach acid. I'm a definite mess. On the other hand, I'm alive.>

<Yeah,> I said. I reared up to my full height and took a look around. I could tell that we had run up into the mouth of a river.

The riverbanks were steep on our side of the river. My pathetically dim bear vision could barely make out some vague shapes moving on the far bank. I sniffed the air. The grizzly sense of smell is excellent. What I smelled was puzzling. <I'm smelling . . . I don't know what. It's like something is missing. Like the air has been scrubbed clean. I smell various trees and plants,

but . . . > I shook my huge head. <I don't know. Something I should be smelling, only I'm not.>

Tobias stood up shakily on his talons. <Car exhaust? The smell of fossil fuels burning? The faint smells of backyard pools and grease-belching fast-food restaurants? The smell of human sweat, perfume, garbage? In other words, all the smells of civilization?>

<Yeah. Exactly. You're right.> I glared at him. <Too right. How did you know? What's going on, Tobias?>

<Well, my wings and tail are a mess, but my eyes are still working. I can see what you can't.>

<You can't *see* smells.>

<No. But I can see that small herd over across the river. That small herd of hadrosaurs over there.>

<What is a hadrosaur?> I demanded. I was getting annoyed at the way Tobias sounded. Like he was about to say something important, only he couldn't quite spit it out.

<Hadrosaurs were a group of duck-billed dinosaurs.>

<Tobias, would you mind making just a little bit of sense? Dinosaurs?>

<Yeah. And let's see, if I remember my old dinosaur books, those long-necked things in the water were Elasmosauruses and the thing that

you just chewed a hole through was probably a Kronosaurus.>

<Yeah. Right.> I waited for him to laugh at his own joke. Only he didn't laugh. <Dinosaurs?>

<Yeah. Dinosaurs.>

<Oh, man. Tobias, we are gonna need some better morphs.>

CHAPTER 9

Tobias

I was in pain. I didn't want to mention it, though. What was the point?

I had very few morphs, unlike the others. We were on land now. A dolphin morph wasn't any use. The only useful morph I had was my human one.

But somehow a human body seemed pathetically weak in a world of dinosaurs. At least in my own hawk body I could fly away from danger.

Unfortunately, my hawk body was a mess.

<Now what do we do?> Rachel wondered. <What about the others? Do you think they made it?>

<I don't know.> I tried to extend my broken wing. <Ahh!>

<Does it hurt?>

<Not really,> I lied.

High above me the huge bear head looked down at me. <Why don't you morph to human, then morph back to your bird body? The new hawk body will be constructed from the DNA and should be fine. Just like what happens when we injure a morphed body.>

<Okay.>

It felt weird going human. I'd only done it a few times since the Ellimist had given me back my morphing power.

Now I felt my feathers itching as they melted into flesh. My sight grew dim, my hearing became muddy. I rose up, tall, large, clunky, awkward . . . human.

"At least the pain is gone now," I said. "Now to get feathery again."

A few minutes later, I was my normal — okay, my abnormal — self. Unfortunately . . .

<Aaaaahh! Oww! It just hurts worse!>

<This makes no sense!> Rachel said, sounding outraged.

I laughed grimly. <Rachel, in case you haven't noticed, our lives stopped making sense that day we walked through the construction site and had a spaceship land in front of us. Maybe it's some effect from the time travel — if that's what's happened to us. I'll be sure and ask Ax, if

we ever see him again. Or maybe the Ellimist messed me up when he gave me back my powers. It'd be a relief to think that guy is capable of screwing up.>

<Then morph to human. We have to get going. Don't ask me where.>

<No. I need to heal. That will take time. I have to stay in my own body for it to heal. But first I need you to set my broken wing.>

<What? I'm not Cassie!>

<You've seen her do it. So have I.>

<Oh, man,> Rachel moaned. <What am I going to use for bandages?>

<Part of your morphing outfit. That and some twigs.>

<Oh, man,> Rachel said again. <I wish Cassie were here.>

She began to demorph. The massive shoulders and head, the lumbering haunches, the shaggy fur, the huge, powerful paws, all shrank and melted. Gradually a very beautiful human girl emerged.

Rachel looked down at her morphing outfit. It was a black, one-piece leotard. "Okay, so I go to the bare midriff look," she said.

She tried to tear a hole in the fabric. "My fingernails are too short."

<Here. Bend down.> She bent close and I used my beak to make a tear in the fabric.

From that first tear Rachel quickly ripped off three strips of black nylon. "I just have one thing to say, Tobias. Don't break another wing. I mean, this doesn't look bad — it could actually be kind of a fashion statement — but any more and we'd be getting embarrassing."

<Hey, I'm a hawk, remember? I would never even look.>

"Yeah, right." She gathered up some twigs that had been deposited along the river's edge. "What do you think? These okay?"

<Should be. Now, look, all you have to do is straighten out my wing. Make sure the bone is lined up straight. Otherwise it'll heal crooked and I'll spend the rest of my life flying around in circles.>

Rachel looked alarmed.

<Just a joke, Rachel,> I said. But silently I added, *I hope.*

She took my broken wing very gently. "I can tell where it's broken. I'll straighten it, then put a stick on each side and tie it up, right?"

<Yep. Nothing to it.>

Rachel took a deep breath. "On the count of three. One . . . two . . ."

<Aaaahhh!> I yelled, as sharp pain shot up my wing.

"Sorry! Sorry!" she cried.

<Just get it over with!> I yelled.

She held the bone in place with one hand. It hadn't broken into separate pieces, it had just snapped. But it was agonizing. No matter how she tried, she couldn't keep from bending the bone slightly.

She grabbed the two sticks with her left hand and managed to line them up against the bone. She transferred the pressure to her left hand and there came a new wave of pain, so severe it made me sick inside.

She quickly wound one strip around my wing.

<Tighter,> I said.

"It'll hurt you."

<It'll hurt worse if my wing doesn't heal.>

She tightened and I tried not to scream.

The other two strips went on easier. She checked the knots, then sat back and wiped her face with the back of her hand. She was sweating and pale.

"I don't know how Cassie does things like that," she said.

<You did great. No training, no experience. Come on, you did great.>

She stood up, and for the first time with decent eyes, looked across the river at the small hadrosaur herd. "Oh, my God. What is this, *Jurassic Park*?"

<Probably more like Cretaceous Park. I think hadrosaurs were more common in the Cretaceous Period.>

Rachel glared at me. "I've known you a long time, Tobias. I don't remember you ever talking about dinosaurs."

<I was so into dinosaurs when I was little,> I said. <I was staying with my uncle at that point. He liked to drink. He'd sit in his La-Z-Boy and start yelling at the TV and cursing, and then yelling at me if I made any noise. I used to go into my room and sit there, playing dinosaur.>

We started to climb up the bank of the river. Or to be more accurate, Rachel started to climb, and I perched like so much dead, useless weight on her shoulder.

It was a struggle to hold on without digging my talons into her skin. I'm sure I hurt her. But Rachel, being Rachel, said nothing.

We reached the top of the bank. We were in a sea of grass that extended alongside the river-bank. Beyond the grass was a line of dark, forbidding trees. Here and there I saw flashes of color: flowers. And then there was the volcano.

<Flowers,> I said. <Cretaceous Period.>

"So what's the difference between Jurassic and Cretaceous?"

<Well, a lot of things. Cretaceous was the last age of dinosaurs. They died out very suddenly at

the end of the age, about sixty-five million years ago. I mean, well . . . sixty-five million years before our own time.>

"So in the Cretaceous Age there's probably just the leftover dinosaurs. Not like the ones in *Jurassic Park*."

<Not exactly,> I said. <See, *Jurassic Park* was slightly inaccurate. I mean, some of the dinosaurs they showed were actually from *this* time, from the Cretaceous.>

She looked hard at me. "You're not going to tell me what I hope you're not going to tell me, are you?"

<Afraid so. If I'm right and we are in the Cretaceous Period, well then, this is the age of the most relentless, powerful, dangerous, ruthless predator in all of history. This is the age of Tyrannosaurus rex.>

CHAPTER 10

Marco

CRASH! CRASH! CRASH!

The ground shook!

"HrrrrRRROOOOAAAARRR-unh!"

It was so loud it had to be right behind me! I was screaming. I was crying as I ran. It was panic. Pure panic. Leaves slapped my face. Twigs whipped my bare arms.

I glanced back. Through my blurring tears I saw it bounding, leaping, running after us.

Forty feet long, from head to tail. Twelve thousand pounds. Seven-inch, serrated-edged teeth.

But it was the eyes that were the worst. They were intelligent, eager eyes. Hungry eyes. Eyes that seemed almost to laugh at me, helpless creature that I was.

Could I morph? Morph what? Morph *what*? There was nothing that could stand against a Tyrannosaurus rex. Nothing! My gorilla morph? The Tyrannosaurus would eat it in two bites.

I saw flashes of the others, all in flat-out panic run. It would have us all. None of us could fight it. Not even Ax, who was pulling ahead of the stumbling humans.

No! Wait! There was a way!

"Get small!" I screamed. "Morph small!" The words tore my throat as I yelled.

Wham!

The root seemed to reach up out of the ground to grab my foot. I hit hard. I sucked air but nothing came. My lungs were emptied. Heart pounding. The others kept running. Didn't realize I'd fallen. Roll!

I rolled over just as the impossibly big talon came raking down.

WHAMMM! The tyrannosaur's foot hit like a dropped safe. I bounced from the impact.

Down came the head, teeth flashing, eyes greedy for my flesh.

I sucked in a breath. Rolled, scrambled, tripped, kicked forward and landed in a fern at the base of a tree. The tree trunk was no more than a foot in diameter.

I pulled myself behind it. No way to hide.

The dinosaur kicked at me with one foot. I dodged.

"Morph, you idiot!" someone yelled at me. I recognized my own voice, but I couldn't imagine speaking the words.

What? What could I morph? What was small enough?

SCRRRRRAACK! WHAAAMMM! A talon came down and scraped the bark off the tree before it hit. I yanked my leg out a split second before it would have been crushed.

Talon? Yes, huge bird feet. Bird, that was the trick. See if the big, evil creep could fly!

I focused some part of my mind on the image of an osprey. Small, too small for the T-rex to care about. And it could fly.

I felt the changes begin, but the Tyrannosaurus hadn't gotten to be the biggest flesh-eater in history by being stupid. It came around the tree for me. And now my body was growing clumsy as my hands shrank and my legs thinned.

You have no concept of how powerful that Tyrannosaurus was. You cannot possibly even begin to understand till you've cowered beneath it, peeing in your pants, and wanting to dig a hole in the dirt.

I scrambled around the tree. Jaws opened four feet wide and snapped shut an inch from my head.

"Aaaahhhh!" I screamed in sheer terror.

The big lizard dodged the other way and it roared in frustration. He was so close I felt the sound waves. I saw his pebbly-skinned throat vibrate. And worse, I saw into his mouth. A mouth glittering with teeth like butchers' knives and stained with the blood of his last kill.

I scrambled away again, stiff, barely able to move.

CRUNCH!

The Tyrannosaurus chomped its jaws shut on the tree itself. He began to twist and rip the tree, like a dog with a bone. Rending, tearing, bark flying, white wood pulp chewed to chips.

In a few seconds the tree would no longer be between us. And already I was too far morphed to run to another tree.

"Grrr-UNCH! Grrr-UNCH! Scree-EEEEEEEE-crrUNCH! RrrrOOOAAAARRR!"

The Tyrannosaurus had gone mad with frustration. It was screaming in rage, ripping, grinding, throwing its huge weight back and forth. Shaking the ground. Bruising the air with its insane roar. Just a few seconds more and . . .

Crrr-SNAP!

The tree fell slowly away, crashing down through layers of vines and ferns.

The Tyrannosaurus lunged, mouth open, red tongue lolling, teeth wet with drool.

I tried to leap back. I fell. Rolled. Thrashed, out of control.

Wings! I had wings!

Too late!

The mouth came down over me like some kind of earthmover, like a diesel shovel. A prison of teeth all round me. The jaw bit into the dirt itself. A root! Teeth snagged by a root. I flapped, ran, beat, rolled, scrambled.

Out between the jaws!

Running on osprey talons, running, wings open, flapping.

SNAP! Jaws an inch behind my tail.

Fly, fly, fly you idiot!

Bonk.

I never saw the tree trunk. I hit it head-on. I was stunned, senseless, helpless.

The Tyrannosaurus roared in triumph.

It towered above me, huge, irresistible. Pure destruction. *Why had it chased me?* I wondered. Why? I was too small, wasn't I?

But of course. I'd been in predator morph before. I knew why. Because killing was what it did. Killing was what it was. It had gone beyond food or hunger now. It simply wanted to do what it did best.

I flapped weakly, too dazed to move.

Down came the head. Down from so far above. Down it came.

A swift movement to my right. What was it?

Fwapp! Fwapp! Fwapp!

An Andalite tail, too fast to be seen, struck three times.

The dinosaur swung its head hard. Ax went flying and rolled twice as he hit the ground.

The T-rex sagged. Tried to roar. And fell.

Human hands snatched me up as six tons of malevolence fell to the ground.

CHAPTER 11
A x

I wiped my tail blade on some large leaves. Unfortunately, more than my tail was stained.

My human friends were all looking at the big creature. Marco was becoming human again. I was busy trembling.

"Nice work, Ax," Prince Jake said. He slapped his hand on my shoulder. It is a thing humans do to indicate friendship or congratulations. Sometimes they do it to kill small insects called mosquitoes.

<I was toast,> Marco said, still more osprey than human. <You saved my life, man.>

<I was fortunate,> I said.

"I can't believe you took that monster down," Prince Jake said.

<Prince Jake, please don't think I can fight and defeat these creatures. This animal was busy chasing Marco. It was distracted. It is not accustomed to being attacked.>

"You're just being modest," Cassie said.

<No!> I said, more sharply than I'd intended. <Listen to me: I know my capabilities. In face-to-face, one-on-one combat, that creature would have destroyed me. One-against-one I will lose ninety percent of the time.>

"Oh," Prince Jake said.

"Yeah, well, you came through big time on this go-round," Marco said. He held his hands out straight. They were trembling. "I can't stop shaking."

"This is insane," Cassie said. She looked around carefully. Peering cautiously, looking, no doubt, for others of the big creatures. "What is going on? Why are there dinosaurs here? Where is *here*?"

<Is there not some place on your planet where this creature lives?>

She shook her head violently. "No. Not in millions of years, anyway. Tens of millions, probably. No, there is no place on Earth where tyrannosaurs just run around in the woods."

"Yeah, I think we'd have heard about it in school," Marco said. I believe his tone of voice indicated something the humans call "dry humor." I have not heard any wet humor, so it is difficult for me to tell the difference.

My immediate terror was fading. A deeper pessimism was setting in. It was easy to see that humans — or Andalites — deprived of the power of civilization were pathetically weak in this environment.

"Some kind of real-life *Jurassic Park*?" Prince Jake speculated. "Maybe someone actually did it. You know, cloned DNA from old dinosaur bones."

<That is scientifically possible,> I said. <But I have been feeling a strange distortion in my time-keeping sense. This planet is no longer rotating at the same speed as before. I think the likely explanation is that we have traveled a very, very long way in time.>

Prince Jake raised one eyebrow and looked at me. "Millions of years?"

<Once a *Sario Rip* — a time-rift — is created, there is no difference between a year and a million years. The energy required is the same. I think I remember the equations . . . in an equation where t is time, z is Zero-space, w inversely cubed represents the nexus of —>

"Uh-uh," Marco said, raising his hand. "You saved my life. Don't undo it by killing me with algebra."

<I'm not an expert, of course. We studied the

66

Sario effect in school. But I may not have been paying very close attention. Who knew I'd ever need to understand time-rifts?>

"How do we get back?" Cassie asked.

<I don't know. There is no way of duplicating the event that created the *Sario Rip*. That explosion in the submarine.>

"What? You can't just whip up a fusion bomb?" Marco said.

<Fusion bomb?> I asked. Then I laughed. I knew I shouldn't, but you have to admit, it was funny. <A *fusion* explosive? That's what it was? I assumed it was a small proton-shift weapon, at least. Fusion is only used in children's toys. You know, to make the little dolls speak and so on.>

My human friends stared at me.

"So the Andalite Toys 'R' Us must be a wild place, huh?" Marco said.

"Let's focus here," Prince Jake said impatiently. "Rachel and Tobias may have been killed. In any case, there's nothing we can do about it. We are millions of years in our own past, and there's nothing we can do about that. We're in the age of dinosaurs, and none of our morphs can even begin to fight things like . . ." He jerked his thumb at the massive corpse. ". . . like that. So the question is: What do we do?"

Prince Jake had summed up the situation very well. We were trapped in an exceedingly dangerous world where we could do almost nothing to defend ourselves.

I turned my stalk eyes toward the Tyrannosaurus's head. The mouth was partly open. The sight of those teeth made my insides watery all over again. I could see the serration on the back side of the teeth. Like shark teeth, only much, much bigger.

I had a clear mental picture of what would have happened if the creature had turned a little faster to confront me. The jaws closing over the upper half of my body . . . a violent shake of the head to rip me into easy-to-swallow pieces . . .

"We adapt," Cassie said grimly. "That's what animals have to do in order to survive. Our environment is massively different. No civilization to rely on, surrounded by brutal predators. So we adapt. Or we get eaten."

"Great. *Robinson Crusoe* meets *Jurassic Park*. Look at us. We have nothing," Marco said. "No homes. No food. No tools. No weapons. We don't even have shoes!"

"Well, we're going to have to make all those things," Prince Jake said. "And we do have one big weapon: We can still morph. Maybe we can't fight a T-rex, but we can fly, and we can escape."

"We have food and shoes right here," Cassie said. She was looking at the dead Tyrannosaurus. "Ax has his tail. We can use the hide to make sandals. Skin from the lower leg there looks pretty tough and thick. We cut out some skin, remove the meat and eat it. Then we use ligaments and tendons to lace up the sandals."

I believe Prince Jake and Marco were shocked. Humans are strangely squeamish at times. I can never predict when.

"Wow," Marco said. "Wow. You're kind of getting into this, aren't you, Cassie?"

Cassie walked up to the dinosaur and placed one hand on its leg. She tested the skin with her fingertips. "Look, Marco, my best friend is gone. Tobias is gone. I don't want any more names added to that list. We need food. There's no Burger King anywhere nearby, okay? We're not big or mean enough to be predators in this environment. We've moved way down on the food chain. The best we can be is scavengers. Here's thousands of pounds of protein. We eat some now, and we smoke some for jerky so we can eat later."

If anything, Prince Jake and Marco appeared even more shocked. And I felt the same. This was an aspect of Cassie I'd never seen. But then, Cassie is more involved than the others in the facts of environment. She had sized up the situation and realized that in this new world she and her fellow humans were no longer masters.

I began to feel a little better about our

chances. Humans may be technologically primitive, not to mention physically weak, what with tottering around on two spindly legs. But if you're in a situation that requires instant adaptability to change, you should always have a couple of humans along with you.

Cassie looked at me, making eye contact with my main eyes. "Ax, are you okay doing this? Your tail is all we have."

<Yes. I will do all I can.>

"Okay, then. Jake, maybe you and Marco could gather up any dry sticks and dry grass you can find nearby. We have to work fast. We aren't the only animals who'll be after this much meat. Ax? I need you to slice this area of leg into squares, each about one foot square."

I glanced at Prince Jake.

Prince Jake smiled and shrugged. "Cassie's the boss on this," he said. "She has a clue. I don't. And we all know Marco doesn't."

"You got that right," Marco agreed.

I turned all my eyes on the haunch of the dead creature. I took careful aim and began the work.

CHAPTER 12
Rachel

My feet were torn bloody. I was leaving traces of red on the razor-edged saw grass. The legs of my leotard were torn and tattered. It was not a good look. The bare midriff thing, maybe. The fringe look? No.

I was carrying Tobias in my arms. He couldn't fly. He was too slow at walking. And if I carried him perched on my shoulder, no matter how careful he was, the jerking and wobbling would force him to dig his talons into my skin.

Not fun. Especially not fun because the whole time I was expecting some murderous dinosaur to come ripping out of the woods to our left.

<You doing okay?> Tobias asked.

"Sure. No problem," I said, trying to sound cheerful. "I could stand a little less humidity, maybe."

<Yes, it is . . . unh . . . damp.>

His groan of pain made me feel guilty for thinking about my own problems. "Tobias, maybe you should morph to human for a while."

<I'm sorry. You must be getting tired of carrying me.>

"No, no, it's not that. It's just that your wing is hurting you. If you were in human morph, there wouldn't be any pain."

<I can only stay in morph for two hours, Rachel. Then I have to demorph and I'm right back where I started. Plus I won't continue healing during that time. Not to mention the fact you'd have to redo my splint. And that wasn't fun for either of us.>

"You could just stay human. Permanently. There are worse things."

He didn't say anything for a while. When he did speak, it wasn't about morphing. <Can you lift me up for a minute? I think I see something.>

I raised him up high above my head. "What is it?"

<Smoke! I see a column of smoke.>

"Like a forest fire? Or is it that volcano?"

<No, like a campfire!>

I lowered him back down. "Maybe it's the others. Maybe they made it to shore and started a fire. I mean, there are no humans here, right?"

<Not for another sixty or eighty million years,> Tobias said. <Not even monkeys. Not even our most distant relatives. The only mammals around are early versions of rats and shrews.>

I smiled. "If Marco were here he'd make some snide remark about you having plenty to eat, at least."

Tobias laughed. <Yeah. And speaking of which . . .>

"At least we have water as long as we stay by the river. On the other hand, what if that smoke is from Cassie and Jake? We have to go find out. Besides, the sun's going down. We could use a fire."

<You go,> Tobias said. <It looks like it's about two or three miles away. You could morph to your bald eagle body, fly over, take a look, and come right back for me.>

"Yeah, right. Like I'm going to leave you here in the middle of nowhere, helpless."

He argued with me a little. Said he'd be okay and so on. But there was no way. We decided to drink our fill from the river. Then we turned away from it toward the smoke. Already it was harder to see in the fading sunlight.

The saw grass gradually gave way to shorter

grasses. And the forest that had been on our left the whole time receded. We were walking now across a plain that looked like something you'd expect to see lions roaming. But we were tens of millions of years away from lions.

"Lions I could handle," I muttered.

<What?>

"Nothing. Just thinking out loud. Oh, man!"

<What?>

"I have to set you down for a second," I said. I laid him back on the golden, foot-high grass. I began to pick the insects off my feet. Several different species of bugs had been attracted to the cuts on my feet.

<Rachel, why didn't you tell me your feet looked like that?> Tobias cried.

I shrugged. "Looks worse than it is. Besides, this grass we're in now isn't bad."

<You have to take it easy for a while, Rachel. You're going to end up as —>

He fell silent. He cocked his hawk's head left, then right.

"What is it?"

<I hear something. Something large.>

In addition to their amazing sense of sight, birds of prey also hear very, very well. I jumped up, grabbed him, and held him high over my head to give him the best possible view. But the truth is, I could see what there was to see well enough.

I almost dropped him.

Four . . . no five creatures that looked a little like rhinoceroses. Only instead of one horn, they had two hugely long horns protruding from a thick, scalloped shell around their heads.

"Even I know that dinosaur," I said. "Those are Triceratops. But they're just plant-eaters, right? Not dangerous?"

<No, they aren't dangerous,> Tobias agreed. <But what you can't see is the pack of Deinonychus moving in to attack them. *They're* dangerous. But I don't think there are enough of them to go after a Triceratops. The Tri's can make a run for the river, get their backs to it, and the Deinonychus would be out of luck.>

I didn't ask how Tobias could size up the situation so well. Probably because he is a predator. Actually, two kinds of predator: hawk and human. The combination of hawk instincts and human intelligence gives him a lot of insight into the battle for survival.

<Strange. Deinonychus was supposed to have been a smart pack-hunter. But these guys have blown it. Unless . . .>

He turned his head to look behind us and let out a thought-speak moan.

<Score one for Deinonychus. We've screwed up,> he said. <They're behind us. Coming slowly this way in a pincer action to trap the Triceratops.>

"How big do you think they are?"

<Not big. Maybe five feet tall, ten feet long from nose to tail.>

"Big deal. That's only about the size of a big kid or a small man."

<Wrong comparison. That's about the size of a wolf. We're talking very fast, very smart wolves.>

They were close enough now that I could see them, even with my sun-strained human eyes. Man-sized lizards bounding along on powerful legs. Their pebbly skin was the color of asparagus soup and coffee ice cream, swirled together. Not that I was getting really hungry or anything.

A gust of wind ruffled my hair. The wind blew our scent toward the Deinonychus. I saw one of them stop, raise his head, and turn it toward us.

I felt the eyes searching for me. And I swear I felt the moment when those cold, yellow eyes locked onto me.

"Hroooo! Hroooo!" the dinosaur cried.

They broke into a run.

"Uh-oh." I grabbed Tobias and started to run, the pain in my bloody feet forgotten. Stupid. I might as well have been trying to outrun a wolf.

<The other pack is coming after us, too!> Tobias yelled.

Suddenly it wasn't the big Triceratops caught in the Deinonychus's trap. It was a much, much easier prey.

CHAPTER 13

Cassie

"Faster . . . okay, more grass . . . okay, hoooof, hoooof!"

I blew lightly on the dry grass. Jake moved the tendon bow back and forth as fast as he could. Marco held the top of the stick.

It had taken a while for us to piece together old bits of forgotten Boy Scout lore and scenes we'd seen on TV or in movies or read about in books.

But eventually we'd figured it out, starting with a flat piece of wood as a base. Ax cut a small notch in it. We then took a straight stick about a foot long. That we held upright, using pieces of bark to protect the holder's hands from the friction.

We fashioned a bow by stringing a length of

Tyrannosaurus tendon cut from the animal's foot. We put a half loop of the bowstring around the upright stick. Then all we had to do was move the bow quickly back and forth. The vertical stick spun in the groove of the flat base piece. And slowly but surely, the heat of friction began to glow.

I grabbed a tiny handful of dry grass. I bent over, my face just inches away from the base. I added a bit more grass and blew again, gently, gently.

A piece of grass crisped and twisted. More air. I blew harder. More browning, twisting grass. I began to despair.

"Flame!" Marco cried.

It was true. A tiny flame. Very tiny. I fed more grass into it. More grass. Now the tiniest twigs. The twig caught fire!

I looked up at Jake and Marco. Their faces were shining.

"Wow," I whispered. "This is the first deliberately made fire. Ever. We just invented fire."

Ax leaned down low to help pile larger sticks on the flame. It was mesmerizing. The flame grew and grew. It ate up the grass and moved up to the sticks.

I just sat there, feeling weird and significant and yet silly. It was like a holy religious ritual. Man creating fire.

Or in this case, woman, I thought with a grin. Rachel will appreciate . . . . But no, Rachel wasn't around anymore.

Marco stepped away and came back with a long stick. He'd impaled a half dozen shreds of Tyrannosaurus meat on the stick. He held them over the fire.

They crackled and sizzled and smelled wonderful.

I folded my legs and my awkward Tyrannosaurus sandals under me. It was starting to get dark under the trees. But we had fire. We alone, on all of planet Earth, had fire.

We had moved away from the dead dinosaur just as a bunch of very tiny, swift, two-legged dinosaurs showed up looking for a late lunch. We were now camped at the edge of the plain, with the woods fifty yards away at our backs. We'd chosen the spot because there was a stream running by. And because we just didn't know which was safer: open country or woods.

"Okay, who's going to be first?" Marco asked, holding out a strip of hot meat. "We have medium rare and well-done."

Jake reached for the slice. He took a cautious bite.

"Just don't say it tastes like chicken," Marco said.

Jake considered. "It tastes like fish, actually. Like a mild fish. Maybe like swordfish. It could use some salt."

Marco cocked an eyebrow at me. "Now he's a food expert?"

I laughed softly. I took a piece. It was delicious. But then again, I was starving.

"The first cooked food in all of history," Marco observed. "Plus the first complaint about food in all of history. Ax-man, you want to grind a hoof into a piece of this? Or maybe you could morph to human and eat it?"

Andalites eat by absorbing grass through their hooves as they run or walk.

<No, thanks. I've grazed very well.>

Ax was watching the grassy plain. He was using his stalk eyes to swivel carefully in all directions.

The sky was shading from blue to brilliant red and orange, with sunset coming on quickly. A massive, distorted-looking red sun slipped below a layer of high clouds and dropped behind the volcano.

"Beautiful," I said, mostly to myself.

"The first person in history to appreciate a sunset," Marco said.

"How much longer do you figure you'll be doing that, Marco?" Jake asked tolerantly.

Marco grinned. His face was red from the glow of sunset. "The first person to ever complain about someone talking too much."

"What are we going to do about it getting dark?" I asked.

Jake looked surprised. "I don't know. You've been so cool about all this back-to-nature stuff, I guess I was waiting for you to tell us."

Was he resentful that I had been taking a more active role? No. Surely not. "I don't have any brilliant ideas."

"Doesn't fire keep animals away?" Marco asked.

"Not always," I said. "Not predators. In Africa, man-eating lions and leopards go right to villages, into huts and drag people away. In grasslands like this, you get lightning fires all the time. Some of the predators may have learned to let the fire drive smaller prey toward them."

"The first really, really depressing example of way too much information in all of history," Marco said.

"We have our weapons," I said.

Jake said, "Yeah. Three sharp sticks. Plus Ax's tail. Throw in some burning torches and we can probably handle some of the smaller predators."

I felt a chill and scooted closer to the fire, which now blazed up fairly well. The image of a huge T-rex looming up suddenly, gold and red from the firelight, its vast mouth open, eyes greedy . . . I took a couple of deep breaths.

I'm not Rachel. I can't just turn off the fear. If Rachel were here, she'd say something cocky about kicking Tyrannosaurus butt. We'd all know it was just bold talk, but we'd feel better, anyway.

"Okay," Jake said. "We sleep in shifts. Ax's time-tracking sense is messed up, but he can approximate two hours and wake us up. Two of us awake at all times. The people who are awake will sit facing out, away from the fire. That way their eyes will be adjusted to seeing in the dark."

"Good plan," Marco said. "That way there'll be two of us to scream, 'Oh no, we're toast!' when the next Big Rex shows up."

"If a predator shows up, what do we do?" I asked.

Jake considered for a moment. "I think the most dangerous morph any of us has is my tiger morph. If we're attacked, I'll morph. Ax will use his tail. Cassie and Marco, you grab your weapons. The three of you try and hold off the . . . the whatever shows up . . . till I've morphed. An Andalite and a tiger together should be enough. Then Marco and Cassie, you two will morph. But morph something to escape, not fight."

"Cassie and I, we wave sharp sticks at a Big Rex?" Marco asked skeptically. "Meanwhile, you're helpless in mid-morph."

"You have a better plan?" Jake asked testily.

"Sure. If Big Mister T shows up, we scream and cry and blubber like babies till he eats us."

Jake grinned. Then he laughed. So did I. It wasn't even slightly funny, of course, but sometimes fear and exhaustion can combine to make you giddy.

"Okay, Cassie and Ax take the first watch. Marco, you and I have to try and sleep."

"At least I won't have any bad dreams," Marco said. "I'm already in one."

Jake and Marco fell silent. I don't know if they slept at all. I turned away from the fire and looked out into darkness that was deepening with shocking speed. Already the night was rushing toward us out of the east, pushing away the last tendrils of red sunlight.

Then I saw it. Like someone had painted a brush stroke of fairy dust across the sky.

"Ax," I whispered. "Is that a comet?"

<Yes. It is very beautiful.>

"Even to you? You must have seen comets up in space."

<They are most beautiful when they are closest to a star. The star, the sun, is what causes the tail to extend.>

"Oh. Looks close."

<It may be,> Ax said. <It is either very close or very large. My people — a long time ago, of

course — used to believe that comets were omens of bad things that would happen.>

I was surprised. "Really? Humans thought the same thing." Darkness fell. There was no moon in the sky. The starlight never touched the grass sea around us. The firelight was puny.

"Are you scared, Ax?"

<Yes.>

"Me, too."

I felt the stick in my hand. I felt the fire at my back. Little, weak, defenseless Homo sapiens, I faced a night full of terrors.

CHAPTER 14

Tobias

Deinonychus. That's what they were, I was pretty sure. At least, I thought so. I couldn't remember. But learning about dinosaurs in books isn't like seeing them face-to-face.

They were hunting us. Like a wolf pack. They were taking their time because we were unfamiliar prey. A strange creature that ran on two legs while carrying a big bird.

Yes, we were something new. New meat.

Rachel ran toward the spot where the campfire had been before the failing light had rendered the smoke invisible. It had seemed to be coming from the edge of the plain that opened before us. As she ran, I watched the Deinonychus pack. I watched them as a professional predator myself.

Was there communication between them? It sure seemed like the two bands of Deinonychus were moving in concert.

It was a triangle, basically. One group behind and to the west. The second group level with us but to the east. We were running north. If we veered slightly left, we'd hit the edge of the forest. Was that the right move?

<Rachel, head for the woods.>

"Why?" she managed to gasp. Rachel's in shape, but running barefoot while carrying a hawk is not easy.

<They're pack-hunters. I think the two groups can see each other and adjust to each other. Even in this light. In the trees they'll lose their line of sight.>

Rachel didn't say anything. But she did veer left a little. Toward the trees.

I focused my hawk eyes on the westerly group. They were speeding up!

A quick glance to the east. They were speeding up, too, but only after the first group did.

<I thought so,> I said. <The leader of the pack is with that western bunch. I think I know which one it is. He's got about a foot of his tail missing.>

The Deinonychus were running now. They were quite fast. And so close I could see details of the leader: the pebbly lizard skin, the way the tail stuck out stiff as a board for balance, the placid expression on that intelligent face.

His weapons were formidable. He stood no taller than a short man or a tall boy. But his jaw could close over a human head. His hands were relatively larger and stronger than a Tyrannosaurus's, with wicked, down-curved claws. But it was the feet that were the main weapon. They were talons, not so very different from my own. But on each foot there was an upraised claw, seven, eight inches long. It reminded me of Ax's tail blade. That claw, kicked by that coiled steel leg, would slice through a car door.

<We'll reach the woods before them,> I said. <But then we have to act quickly. We have to separate.>

"No way!"

She assumed I was being self-sacrificing. <Rachel, look. They're after *you*, not me. I have a plan.>

She said nothing. Just gasped and panted. I could hear her heart pounding madly.

Trees! We hit the tree line and suddenly it occurred to me just how late in the day it was. The sun was setting in a blaze of glory out on the plain, but under the trees it was already night.

<Stop right here.>

Rachel stopped. She dropped me in the dead leaves. She bent over double, hands on her knees, throwing up from exhaustion. The predator in me was glad. Perfect. The powerful, unfamiliar scent would draw the Deinonychus right to this point.

<Okay, I can't fly, but I can grip. I want you to throw me. Straight up. Up into this tree. Up to that branch.>

"Wha . . . wha . . ."

<Rachel, don't argue. Throw me. Then run and do your bear morph. It may buy you time.>

Besides, I added silently, *you don't want to die as helpless prey. As a human, you'll simply be ripped apart. You'll be eaten alive. As a bear, they'll at least have to fight you first.*

Rachel stood up. Then she bent over, cramped in her right side. She winced in pain. I could see her feet were torn. She was exhausted. But not beaten yet. When she met my gaze, I still saw fierce Rachel in her blue eyes.

<We have to do this now,> I said. <They'll be here in less than a minute.>

"Okay." She reached down and lifted me up. Like someone heaving a basketball from her chest, she threw me upward. Too low! I missed the branch. I flapped my wings, an instinct. A painful, searingly painful, instinct. I hit the ground.

"I can't do it."

<Do it!>

She grabbed me again. This time she put her whole body into it. Up! The branch. I flapped my good wing, spun in the air, grabbed. Yes. I grabbed with my second talon and held firm.

<Now, run! Run!>

She ran. At least, she hobbled and staggered away through the trees. And I waited. I waited and tried not to think of what would happen to Rachel if I messed up.

My branch was just six feet above the ground. I felt totally helpless. I was a bird who could not fly. And there is nothing weaker than a bird who can't fly.

I gripped my branch. Noises. Many clawed feet running. A Deinonychus appeared. Its tail was minus about a foot of length. The leader of the pack.

"Heeeeessss!"

He froze. He looked at the mess Rachel had left. But he did not walk under my branch. Then another Deinonychus. This one ran right over and sniffed curiously. He had a jagged scar two feet long down his back. I could see it clearly.

Short-tail turned away. Scar walked beneath me. His head was just a foot below me.

Now!

I dropped. I opened my talons. I sank them into reptilian skin, right along the old scar.

"Hrroooohhh!"

The Deinonychus turned his head to glare at me with one eye. He opened a mouth lined with ridiculously large teeth.

I almost lost it. I had to fight the urge to flap away, broken wing and all.

Focus, Tobias, I told myself. I locked the fear out of my mind. I held tight with my talons. And I focused on the dinosaur.

It may have been sixty-five or seventy or eighty million years B.C., but DNA was still DNA.

CHAPTER 15

Tobias

I acquired the Deinonychus. I absorbed his DNA into me. And he grew passive and calm, like most animals do when being acquired.

When I was done he wandered away, as if he'd forgotten what he'd been doing.

I stood there, utterly vulnerable on the forest floor. And then I heard a roar. Not a saurian roar, but the full-throated roar of a very large mammal.

Rachel!

I focused my mind again. I pictured the Deinonychus in my mind. And slowly at first, then faster, the changes began.

All right, Tobias, keep your mind strong! I warned myself. It was a new morph. I'd have to deal with the Deinonychus's instincts.

92

My feathers began to stiffen and harden. It was as if someone were coating them with rubber cement or something. The feather pattern remained at first, but they were glued down. And then they began to melt together.

My beak began to extend, out and out, and at the same time the edges became serrated, almost like a saw. And each saw tooth grew and extended, longer and longer, to begin to form the teeth of the Deinonychus.

All the while I grew. Up and up. From standing a foot tall to five times that height.

My tail feathers twined and twisted together and then my tail hardened and grew. Out and out, impossibly long!

Everywhere I could feel the muscles bulging and growing. Layers of muscle over thickening bones. I rose high on legs like steel springs. My talons became less graceful and more deadly. I found I could raise the huge, killing claw. Yes, that's how I would run, with that claw raised so that nothing would dull its razor-sharpness.

I loved that claw. I pictured it ripping open . . . no! Already the dinosaur's instincts were struggling to rise up in my own mind.

But that wasn't going to happen. It *couldn't* happen. Rachel needed me.

But the power! The vivid, electric energy in every cell of my body!

My eyesight grew dim. But not much worse than human eyes, and better in that they could see fairly well in the dark. My hearing diminished, but again, not by much. And to compensate for those losses, the sense of smell flooded my consciousness.

What?

What smell was that?

I stood up and sniffed the wind.

"Roooooaaarrrr!" a deep, hoarse voice bellowed.

"Heeeessss! Heeeesss!" A more familiar cry.

The hunt was on! The pack had cornered its prey. I had to hurry. Hurry, or all the best meat would be taken. I'd have nothing but cold carrion.

With my mouth watering, I bounded away, tearing through the underbrush to join the pack.

CHAPTER 16
Jake

I woke up. It was dark. I was all hot on the side near the fire and cold on the other side. I heard the gurgling of the stream. I'd been dreaming of home. In my dream I was eating dinosaur-shaped cereal at the breakfast table with my parents.

I didn't want to think about my parents. What they would be going through worrying about me just made me sick to my stomach.

"Have you seen anything?"

"Yaaahhh!" Cassie yelped. Then, "Good grief, you scared me."

Marco moaned in his sleep.

I rubbed my eyes. I could not believe I had

actually fallen asleep. But obviously I had. "Ax, how are you doing?"

<I am well. My time-sense has returned fully. It takes a while to calibrate for the rotation of a planet. This planet rotates differently than it does in our own time.>

"How long was I asleep?"

<Approximately one of the current hours and fifty-two minutes.> He came close and tossed another piece of wood on the fire.

I stretched out my foot and poked Marco. He moaned again. Then he sat up. "Oh. So it wasn't a dream. Too bad."

"Cassie, you and Ax can —" I stopped. I had looked up at the sky. "What is that?"

"It's a comet," Cassie said. "Isn't it absolutely beautiful?"

"Yeah. Looks awfully close." I gazed up at the sweep of bright dust trailing from the brilliant head.

<It is. In the last three hours it has grown noticeably larger.>

I glanced over at Ax. He was outlined against the stars, a dark shadow with stalk eyes turning restlessly. "It's not going to hit us or anything, is it?" I laughed when I said it.

<I don't think so. First of all, the odds against any particular comet hitting a particular planet are very large. Millions to one at the very least.

Especially since Earth is not large enough to exert much of a gravitational pull. Besides, the comet is now so close and moving so quickly, I have been able to keep track of a rough trajectory. It will be very close. No more than one or two diameters of Earth, perhaps. But I believe it will miss.>

"Well, that's a relief," Marco said. "I wouldn't want to get killed by a comet and cheat the dinosaurs out of eating me."

"You two get some sleep," I said to Ax and Cassie. "Marco and I will take over. But actually, first I have to . . . um . . . I have to take a little walk."

I left the cozy glow of the fire and headed into darkness. Twenty feet, and the fire already seemed like part of some different world. It was so dark. I looked back and it was as if the fire and the comet were both floating in the same empty space.

I did what I had to do, then I saw it. A flash! A sudden flash of light. Low on the horizon to the north. Was it a meteorite? A falling star?

No. There it was again. Faint. A tiny stab of red light. Again. Again.

I hurried back to the others. "Look to the north. Do you guys —"

A flash like the sun exploding! High overhead.

The flash lit up the entire landscape for just

an instant. But in that instant I saw them: a herd of vast creatures. They stood on four tree-trunk legs. They had tremendously long necks and tails that were just as long. It was impossible to know their actual size, but they had to stand at least four or five times my own height. And from head to tail they had to be forty feet.

I'd seen at least ten of them moving toward us along the line of the stream.

And in that same flash of light, the huge dinosaurs had seen something, too. Coming up behind them, on their trail, like a monster in the night, a Tyrannosaurus.

Boom! Boom! Boom! Boom!

The big dinosaurs bolted, breaking into a panicked run. Straight for our camp!

"What was that flash?" Cassie cried as I ran for the fire.

"Everybody run!" I yelled. "It's a stampede."

"Stampede? What is this, a cowboy movie?!" Marco demanded incredulously.

"MOVE!"

Boom! Boom! Boom! BOOM! BOOM! BOOM!

It was like the worst thunderstorm in history. Creatures five times the size of elephants were stampeding. Every step of those big feet was like a pile driver.

"Get across the stream!" I yelled.

"Where is it?"

"What stream?"

"Just follow me."

I ran, making sure Cassie and Marco were keeping up. Ax, I didn't have to worry about. He was far faster than any of us.

The thunder grew louder. All around us. I saw a vast bulk beside me, blocking out the stars. The panicked herd was all around us.

"HRRRROOOOOAAAARRRR!"

My knees turned to jelly. I tripped. I hit hard. The wind was knocked out of me.

A massive, taloned foot landed inches from my head. I rolled. I slammed into a tree trunk. No, the leg of the long-necked dinosaur.

"ScreeeEEEEE!" the terrified animal cried as the Tyrannosaurus bent low. I saw teeth glittering in moonlight. I saw a glowing yellow eye. I heard the chomp of the Tyrannosaurus's jaws as they clamped down.

I was beneath the long-necked dinosaur as it fought. If I'd stood up and stretched, I would have just reached its belly. Tree-trunk legs pounded around me in a frenzy. And all the while the two animals roared and screamed and bellowed in terror and rage.

I covered my ears and screamed. A battle of giants right above me. I couldn't see anything but darkness blotting out stars and the faintest outline of a creature the size of a whale.

I was a cockroach being hunted with sledge-hammers. The ground jumped and slammed into me with each impact. I couldn't even see the legs scuffling and pounding. At any second one would crush me. I curled up in a ball and tucked my head down and shook.

What morph did I have to fight these titans? Nothing. This wasn't my world. I was nothing in this world. All my powerful morphs were nothing in this world.

"ScreeeEEEEE-uh. ScreeeEEEEE-uh!"

"Huh-huh-RoooAAAARRRR!"

A final cry of the big dinosaur ended in a gasp and a collapsing rattle.

The Tyrannosaurus had won. The long-necked dinosaur was done for. Nothing left but for him to fall. Nothing left but for him to drop down onto me.

**Don't miss out on the rest
of the exciting story
coming soon in PART II of
In the Time of Dinosaurs!**